In memory of Jean-Pierre Giordaningo

Teacher, Artist, Friend

# The Boy and the Wolf
## and other stories

By Jérôme Turcan

FIRST EDITION

ISBN:1495968448

# Contents

# The Boy and the Wolf

A powerful wind swept the plain, howling like a giant wolf. In the wilderness, the alerted creatures burrowed, fighting an unequal fight against the fangs of Cold.

It came with snowy footprints. For long months, it had been leaving its immaculate trace. Its breath flowered over the freezing water. It had come in all its deadliness, and life had only to adapt to it rhythms. Fields, forests, villages... all were deserted. The white reaper had played his injustice, imposed his cruel law.

The wind stopped. Families, huddled around their fires in their country homes, trying to escape the teeth of ice, grew aware of the thick dull silence outside. A chill ran through down their spines. In their hearts they nostalgically dreamed of warmer weather.

This hard season had hit precociously, abruptly, the blade of ice surprising all living things. Only the torrential river had resisted that unstoppable adversary, lapping relentlessly against his banks of mountainous snow with tongues of lively water. But soon enough, the streams feeding him froze, and he relented. As the tumultuous rush calmed, the struggle died down, and the surface covered over with ice. Then, all toppled into an icy totality, into the whitened depths of Winter.

Then the wind came back. It swelled, rolling over land and forest, overwhelming with its frozen gusts everything standing in its path, insinuating itself everywhere, with force, whistling. Shattering like a battering ram against trees weakened by the intense white force, the wind blew harder, blew colder yet, over the snowy vastness, a cutting blizzard of glacial crystal.

With these last thrusts in this latest assault, in a starving band, the wolves arrived.

The wolf leader knew instinctively that nearness to mankind was harmful. Stamped into his animal memory, he remembered companions that had disappeared after a loud noise. His nostrils still held that stinging odor from that time, floating through the air with the hotter and more familiar odors of blood, and death.

He and his band were surprised by the brutality of this great cold; they had no choice but to follow their prey. Then, dragged along by their hunger, they penetrated very far toward the south... too far, too near men, within smell of them.

But his pack followed him, and he had their confidence. The cubs were starving; from the eyes of his faithful companion, a regard of trust. The leader knew: we must survive, the pack must eat.

A new day came to the frozen plain. Snow-laden clouds passed in the rhythm of the powerful wind. In the calm of night, their white flakes had amassed again, their thick mantle covering homes and nature.

Head bent low, eyes shut, the man was thinking, his hands closed around a bowl of bouillon for warmth. With a small movement of his hands he would bring the boiling liquid to his lips, and drank slowly, small sips, his eyes still closed as if to keep the heat from escaping through them. When the bowl was finally empty, he set it down. He got up and went to the fireplace, near the fire. He sat down slowly, eyes fixed on the blaze.

Never before in man's memory had the wolves come so near. Of course, it was also true that the winter had never been so hard. But the problem remained: even armed, every trip was dangerous. The distance from one farm to another was great, and even greater was the distance from farm to village. A thick, uniform layer of snow hid the roads, hiding, like so many traps, each pothole, each large rock, making straight roads out of curved ones, making firm ground out of a ditch. What would happen to someone if he were immobilized by a broken axle, caught in the numbing embrace of that cold, confronted with a wolf pack? How many beasts would you be facing? My God, why were they so near? And the children? The children! At that thought, a shiver shook the man, pulled him from his torpor, and with a sudden fear he hurried out, looking for his son.

Wrapped from head to foot in mounds of sweaters and long underwear, Little Francois at four years old looked like a ball of yarn. He ran, stumbling through the powdery snow drifts that covered the yard behind the house.

Tight in his arms he was carrying a young cat, who, not happy with his adventure, was spitting and clawing to try to escape his unfortunate position. Protected by his thick layers of clothing, the child felt nothing; amused, rather, by what he thought was the kitten's playfulness.

Since he wasn't watching his feet, he soon fell headfirst into the snow. The supple young animal took advantage of his liberty and disappeared, bounding through some brambles. The little boy, laughing at the new game, took off after him.

He searched a long time, making difficult progress in the deep snow. He wasn't laughing any longer, not calling for the cat any longer, not really knowing any longer why he had strayed so far from the house. Soon, he felt very small and very lost, and began to cry, in long hopeless sobs.

Night took him very quickly. She came, black, sudden, with a bite of ice, swirling in, bringing with her as she danced a cloud of frozen snow crystals that made her visible. She slapped the cheeks of the child, drying his tears painfully.

Francois could no longer feel his feet or his numb fingers. The talons of Winter cut through the warm thickness of his clothing. Half unconscious, pleading for protection, he huddled against a large tree. That was when he saw brilliant pairs of little lights moving and shining in front of his eyes. Completely worn out but reassured from the feeling of another's presence, the little boy fell into a deep sleep.

The wolf leader was sated. He had managed to feed his pack. An old stag, tired, betrayed by his scent, had succumbed to the starved hunters, not without putting up a ferocious resistance. Before taking up again their unending wandering, they were resting now with full bellies.

The scent of man approached them. It drifted around, now going away, now coming again. It encircled them, insinuating itself, to suddenly grow faint and disappear. Obeying the instinctual wariness of their species, they sought it out, followed it. Not as they would track a possible prey, but from curiosity: this odor, although human, carried with it none of the aggressive emanations of a hunter: a strong scent emitted from nervous tension, the sweat that comes despite the cold, and the effusion of joyous fear. No, this odor was sweet, fresh, touched with anguish, like that of a wolf cub that discovers the edges of his den without knowing where he is going. The scent filled the air very suddenly, becoming very present to the wolves in each cautious step forward. They soon arrived at the source. Frozen stiff, in refuge at the foot of a tree, the man cub looked at them before falling asleep.

The village was in an uproar. Several groups of young men outfitted themselves in great haste. Little Francois had disappeared, and unconsciously the presence of the wolves was mixed in. As soon as they were dressed, the men grabbed their weapons and were ready. The search for the child was becoming a pitiless mission of revenge; only the father had any hope of finding his son in time.

The road led into the deep, silent forest. With each step forward, blackness closed in behind the little group, feebly lit by the halo of their lights. The men made their way slowly, intimidated by the obscure immensity. Each was well aware of the difficulty of their mission. But all, from the humble to the braggart, from the strongest to the weakest, kept quiet from humility. None of them dared to break the oppressive silence, afraid his voice would show his weakness.

Even their weapons, gripped with whitened knuckles, didn't give them that feeling of courage that they had declared back in the village, volunteering with so much bravado. The hunt was for all of them an ancestral rite, the agonizing but intoxicating emotion of the wait, the release of a savage joy, still latent, of the death blow, the pride in the triumphal return to the village with the game prominently displayed; it had nothing of this spiteful and vengeful hunt whose goal was to save a life at some unknown cost. Now, diurnal creatures in a nocturnal world, they found themselves children again, gripped by a visceral fear of wolves.

Dawn timidly crept in through Winter. A few rays of sunlight, rare and discreet, reflected from the thin crystal crust that covered the snow. Slowly, the morning of Winter drew on its sparkling uniform. In this setting, little François woke gently from within a warmth that belied the surrounding cold. The child tried to get up. At that moment, the ground moved: the wolves, tightly snuggled together around his small body, were waking also. Rubbing his eyes in half slumber, he watched them rise, shake, and, one by one, disappear into the deep dark of the woods. Only a large grey wolf stayed, watching him and sniffing the air in the direction of the sunrise. He turned his head, stared intensely at the boy, then pointed his muzzle toward the sky, let out a deep howl, and then rapidly disappeared after his pack.

Night had been long in passing. The men had split into several groups, but they had not found any trace of wolf or child, the falling snow had certainly erased over all tracks, covering them several times over. Their trek through the deep snow had worn them out. Despite this fatigue and discouragement, they had remained in solidarity, and, though each thought of it, none had spoken of the futility of their search.

Now, broken, done in, with each painful step they made their way silently, miserably, back to the village road. Every moment a dull ache within their hearts reminded them of their defeat, unable even to express it with tears, such was the depth of their fatigue. Only the father of Francois, from the corners of his eyelashes, dropped the silent pearls.

A few timid rays of the sun ran over the new day, a welcome sign that came and warmed up the soul of the group. But a howl broke the peace of the morning, re-ignited the heart of these men, fed the fire of their vengeance with embers of their rage! Forgetting their tiredness, unstoppable and furious they threw themselves in the direction of the savage cry.

Like the crack of a whip, the wolf's voice had hit these men; now they were frothing at the mouth, hate in their eyes, approaching with hands gripping their weapons. The desire, the need to kill, lit their faces. No more thoughts of frozen bodies, heavy legs, fear... all of these accumulated anguishes gave birth to a frenzy of murderous fury. That is how they arrived at the center of a clearing surrounding a large tree.

"Hey"

From the deepest unhappiness is born the most intense joy. At the foot of the large tree, a little four-year-old clapped his hands and laughed.

When his father had him tightly in his arms, the tears flowing over his face this time were of joy. Shouts and gunshots in the air completed the scene of wild celebration. The return to the village was triumphal! Never, ever, would Little Francois be afraid of wolves...

especially one who, hidden in the underbrush of the woods, had the faintest hint of a smile on his muzzle.

# A Strange Dog

I was little then, maybe three or four years old. It was a pretty long time ago, but I remember it very well. My father was a farmer. I still don't know why he chose this place to establish our family. The nearest village was far away and everybody there called our site "The Devils' gate". We were not rich then. I didn't know it at the time, but I understood later, maybe that was one of the reasons he picked the place; most likely the least expensive he could find.

Actually, my parents moved in several years before I was born. All the memories of my youngest age were around our little house and, as little it was, in my heart this house takes the place of the most beautiful palace ever.

With a lot of hard work, and the help of a very small spring, rippling at the bottom of our property, my father grew corn, potatoes and wheat. A peach tree, several apple trees and a grapevine gave us, at the right season, little but succulent fruits. My mother raised some chickens and a pig. This pig used to go on vacation every year before Christmas. It always came back a few months later and I thought, when I grew old enough to think about it, that the vacation was not very good for him because he always lost a lot of weight. On the other hand, it was better like that. If it could stay little all his life, it would escape the menace of finishing his days as sausages in a plate. Pretty smart for a pig, wasn't it?

Every week, on Friday, my father attached his cart to our old mule, Mosquito. After dad filled the cart with what he had to sell—fruits, vegetables, chickens and, during the winter, hats and baskets made of straw—the little convoy left to the village, disappearing at the turn of the road long before the sun showed up.

This story happened on one of these Fridays, in very hot weather-- the kind of weather when the air is so hot that you can't see clearly beyond a few yards.

I was playing in the soft sand, which covers little holes dug by the hard rain that falls once a year in this desert area. Around noon I was always starving, and my mamma, while she finished preparing lunch, used to give me a piece of bread to ease my impatience. This day, the heat woke me up very early in the morning, so early that I almost saw my father before he left. I began to ask for food around mid-morning, hours from lunchtime.

I was getting ready to eat my bread when I saw it for the first time: a dog with long hair and a big tail, which looked at me, and then at my bread, starving to all appearances. I loved dogs, I still do. And this one seemed to actually ask me something: to eat of course, with his big eyes, his head inclined on one side, his long tongue licking his lips.

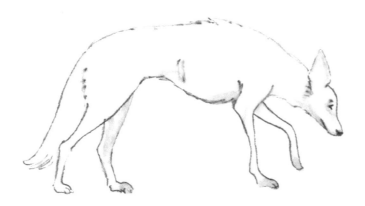

As I said, I loved dogs but I didn't have one. Maybe in my young head began the dream than I could keep this one, who looked neglected. And, as he seemed very shy to me, despite his evident hunger, I went to him and gave him my food. He took it, ran a few yards away and began to eat without stopping to glance at me. Amused by this new game, I went toward him to try to pet his back and make a new friend.

Have I already mentioned that I was pretty lonely around there? After several jumps to dodge me, he stopped and growled, but I was not scared, and too young to be conscious of any danger. So, I went up again and sat in front of him. The dog lowered his ears and closed his eyes, fearful, but he accepted me and let me touch his head.

Encouraged by these first successes, I petted his flank and could feel his ribs. This poor dog was starving! I stood up and went back home.

When my mother saw me she was very surprised. "Already finished?" she asked me.

"Yes!" I had just enough time to answer before going out with a new piece of bread. My dog was still there, where I left him, waiting for me. He ate the bread with the same evident pleasure. After the third run-in and run-out, my mother began to think that it was strange.

"What is going on?" she asked. "What are you doing with all of this bread?" I thought a second and answered with another question, "Can I have some meat now?" She looked at me very suspiciously, but gave me a chicken leg anyway. When I went back to feed my dog again, she followed me. This time, instead a visible desire to take what I brought to him, he surprised me, keeping his distance. A small but perceptible noise behind me told me the reason he was acting like that. My mother, obviously scared, came toward me slowly, trying also to pick up a stick of wood lying on the ground. I understood what she was doing at the same time the dog did and, while he ran away quickly, I screamed at my mother.

"Why did you scare my nice doggy?" She didn't answer, but took my hand and brought me back home, crying.

My father came back early that day. I wasn't sleeping yet. As soon as I saw him I ran in his arms. I was still angry at my mother, and hadn't talked to her all day.

"You look very tired!" said my dad; "Maybe it is time to go to bed, no?" I began to cry, because I wanted to stay with him. While he comforted me, my mother explained the story of the morning to him. When she finished, he looked at me with a big smile.

"Want a doggy?" he asked gently, "Come and see what I brought you from the village…"

I could hardly believe it when he gave me an adorable little puppy. "I was supposed to give you that tomorrow morning, but, if it can console you tonight…"And, with a big smile, glanced at my mother, who still looked upset. "Anyway, even if they are not really dangerous, it's better he plays with a puppy dog instead a coyote!"

# The Good Man Happiness

Once upon a time in a little village lost in the mountains, lived a very old man. He was so old that even the oldest people in town could not remember him any other way. But his age was not the only particularity of the old man. He was also happy, nice, good, and gentle. So happy, nice, good and gentle that everybody used to call him the Good Man Happiness. In fact, nobody could call him by another name since nobody could remember another name for him. And so, for all and everybody, he was The Good Man Happiness. And the old man wore this nickname very well, never making it false. He was nice with cats, he was good with dogs, and he was gentle with birds, always the same and equal to himself, always happy and sharing to everyone his lovely mood. Everybody loved him very much in return and when he came back home, after his daily tour of the neighborhood, he always found his hands and arms full of goodies, flowers and candies. For each, every day he had a good word, a new joke to the men and a smile and a nice complement on the women which was always tasteful.

Very often, all of the gifts he got during his walk made happy some kids or family in greater need than he. He really was a very nice old man. He was the Good Man Happiness.

But, once in his home, alone and out of view of every one, behind his closed doors or by himself in his backyard, which looked somewhat like the Garden of Eden, the old man sometimes worried.

"One more day..." He thought every day when he came back.

"One more day I had the chance to enjoy the beauty of this world. God, thank you. Please make it last. Please, let me see the next day and the next day, always. Let me see, again and again, the smile on the children's lips, the light in their eyes, the happiness on their beautiful faces. Let me please learn the new songs they sing, hear their laughter and their joys. Let me please, help you to make them happy and to always witness their happiness..."

Every day after his little prayer, the Good Man Happiness dried out a small tear in the corners of his eyes and went back to his day and to his work on Earth, making others happy. And it seems that his prayer was heard, because day after day, season after season, year after year, the Good Man Happiness still spread his Joy, his goodies and the gift of his wonderful mood all around him, making the little village the happiest place in all the world.

But the day came that after his words to the Lord, he heard a voice deep in his head. This voice was sweet and the most beautiful he had ever heard. But the words it spoke scared him:

"Good Man Happiness, it is time to leave home. It is time to give to others. The world is vast and people all around it can use a little bit of happiness."

The old man could not move, wondering what was happening to him. After few minutes, he began to think that he just dreamed this, but the beautiful voice came up again:

"Good Man Happiness, you did not dream. You just have time to prepare yourself. Take only a little bag. The road will provide everything you need if you do what you always did. Spread all around you Joy and Happiness."

It took our friend a little time to be able to move again. When he could, he got a little bag and filled it with the most essential items: a handful of happiness, a big and loud laugh, all of the different kinds of smile, a few very good selected jokes and all the love he was capable of, which was almost infinite. He closed the bag and with a light heart, he went to bed where he fell asleep very fast. His dreams were, all night long, full of new faces smiling and laughing around him.

It was dawn still when the door shook under some very loud pounding. The Good Man Happiness was awake in no time. He rolled his cover around him, because he was a little cold despite his pajamas and went to open the door with a bad premonition. Suspicious, he looked from the little window, but didn't see anything, so dark was the early morning. Who could play this kind of joke on him? Reassured with this thought a little bit, he opened the door with a big smile already on his face. His good morning wishes got stuck in his throat. She was here, like he always imagined her. Tall and thin, all dressed in dark with the deepest black stare possible, she was also smiling but her smile was cold and ironic. She was ageless too. Time didn't have any grip on her, but you could say that she was as old as the world, and maybe more. Despite her repulsive appearance, she didn't look mean or cruel. She was above that. She was an important part of life, and used to doing what she had to.

"Good morning, old man. Are you ready to come with me?"

She asked, as if anybody was ever ready to go with a light heart and her voice was the coldest voice he ever heard. Despite the fact that he was very scared and felt uncomfortable, our friend, politely, smiled and answered:

"Good morning to you."

Then, remembering the sweet voice which came to his ear the last evening, he tried to gain some time:

"I wasn't expecting you this early in the morning. Let me get ready…"

His unwelcome visitor cut him sharply with an annoyed voice now:

"Where we go, you will not need anything! Just come with me!"

The Good Man Happiness thought very fast and an idea came to him:

"At least, could I ask you a favor?" He said with the most candid voice possible.

The dark creature inclined her head to the side:

"It is against my principles… And, by the way, why should I allow you a favor? Didn't I give you long enough to do everything you needed to?"

She answered with a very ironic tone. Our friend jumped on the opportunity to make his point.

"Indeed, you forgot me for so long, a few more minutes will not disturb your schedule, and I have to say goodbye to so many of my dear friends…" She stood up angrily; outside the sky became even more dark and threatening.

"I will not let you leave this house, but to follow me!"

He replied with the most reassuring voice he could:

"Oh, no, no, no! I just mean my dear friends in my backyard…"

As she relaxed a bit, he continued:

"…If you promise to let me go three times around my garden, I promise that I will follow you without any more problems or demands." She looked a little confused, and then asked him:

"Why do you want to go three times around your garden, when one would be enough?"

He replied with a tone which begged for compassion.

"Oh please, I have so many friends, it would be so sad to forget even one of them…"

Relieved to close so easy a deal, she agreed:

"Three times only, even if you forget someone! And at the end of the third time…

"At the end of the third time, as I promised, I will follow you."

She gave him her hand to shake. It was the coldest thing he ever touched but at the same time his heart was warm at the thought of his plan…

The Good Man Happiness went for the first time around his garden. He said goodbye to the squirrels, to the deer, to the chipmunk and thanked them for their friendship.

By the pond, he said goodbye to the fish, the frog and the heron, then thanked them for being so long his companions.

He went by the trees and said goodbye to all of the birds, thanking them for the beauty of their songs; and he finished his first time.

Then, he went for the second time around his garden. Now, he said goodbye to each flower and thanked each of them for their wonderful perfumes. He said goodbye to the trees and thanked each of them, one for its fruits, one for its shade during the hot summer. Then, he finished his second time.

After all of these thanks, the old man thought than he could use a glass of water and, very politely, he asked his visitor if she wanted some refreshment. She gave an awful guttural laugh and said:

"Just finish your third turn and hurry, before I lose the little patience I still have!"

The Good Man Happiness smiled gently before entering his home. There, he took a long sip of fresh water, looked around a very last time, gripped his prepared bag and exited his house without looking back.

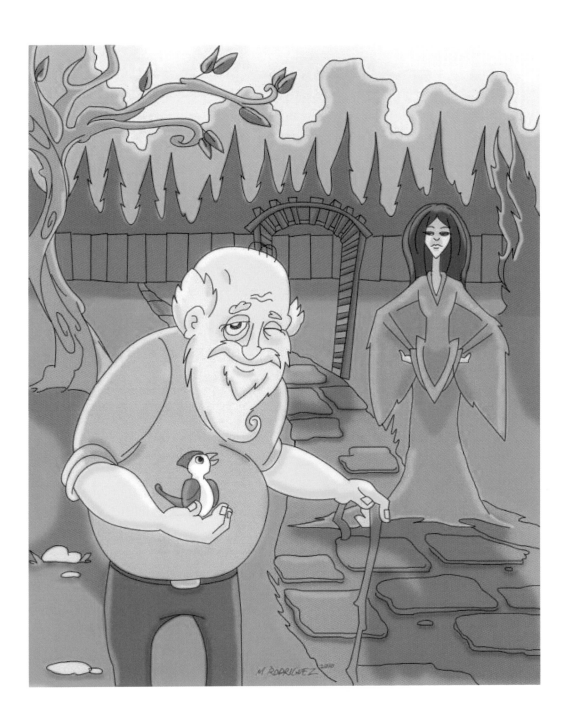

Death waited and waited long before she finally understood that she had been tricked. But she could not do anything about it, since she promised to wait until the end of the third time. Mad with rage, she left at last, frustrated that she would never be able to catch the Good Man Happiness and bring him with her...

As for the Good Man Happiness, he spent his Eternity around the world. He still makes people laugh and smile. He still spreads happiness around him wherever he goes. And every morning when he prays, he does so not to ask anything, anymore, but to thank the Lord for being allowed to continue his job: to make the world a better place to live in.

That is why, despite all the bad things that can happen on Earth, you must keep hope, because happiness is never far, ready to come your way...

The Boy and the Wolf and other stories was written by Jerome Turcan in San Jose, CA, and published by CreateSpace in 2014.

The layout was designed by Jérôme Turcan and Charles Albert.

Illustrations for The Boy and The Wolf by Anthony Albert, Jérôme Turcan and Natasha Turcan.

Illustrations for A Strange Dog by Anthony Albert.

Illustrations for The Good Man Happiness by Mike Rodriguez.